I0562984

My Brother's Keeper:

A Story of Blood and Redemption

Featuring: The Price of Peace

COPYRIGHT

ISBN: 978-0-9965936-6-3

This is a fiction work. Names, characters, places, and incidents are either the product of the author's imagination or are used fictitiously. Any resemblance to actual people, living or dead, or actual events is purely coincidental.

Published by Hayzel Greene

Cover design by Hayzel Greene

Printed in the United States of America

DEDICATION

In loving memory of:

Linda Taylor Fisher "Jeannie" – who always told me I was close to being a genius, and that if I put my mind to it, it could be done.

Willie Demetrius Jones "Bleu" – who showed me life on the other side of the fence.

April Monique Mitchell "Appprreeelll" – who proved that after the tears, there can still be laughter.

Temujin Monroe Hood "P'Nut" – who showed me what true friendship really means.

Charles Taylor "Chawyas Tay" – who taught me the true spirit of a Hip-Hop Head. **Awl Fuckit' Chawyes**

You are all a part of me, and through every word I write, your voices live on.

I dedicate these words in this book to you all for believing in me, pouring into me, and being a part of my journey.

ACKNOWLEDGMENTS

I dedicate these words to everyone who has ever believed in me, poured into me, and walked with me on this journey.

First and foremost, to my mother, **Linda Taylor Fisher** — your love, wisdom, and strength continue to guide me in ways words can't fully capture. Every page I write carries a piece of you.

To my two beautiful daughters — you are my light and my reason. May you always know your dreams are worth chasing and your voices deserve to be heard.

To my friends who left this world too soon — **April, Bleu, and Temujin** — your laughter, encouragement, and belief in me live on in my heart. This book, and every story that follows, carries your spirit between its lines.

To the ones still walking this journey beside me —**Fatimah Pillow Searcy**— thank you for your strength, your laughter, and your constant reminders that art, like love, takes community.

To every reader, supporter, and believer in **The HG Collection** — thank you for reminding me that stories have power when they come from a place of truth.

You have all taught me resilience, reminded me of love's reach, and helped me keep creating when the noise got too loud.

Mr. Brother's Keeper is not just my story, it's a reflection of every lesson, laughter, and memory stitched into this journey.

— **Hayzel Greene**

PROLOGUE
The Weight

"In a world where loyalty costs more than freedom, being your brother's keeper comes with a price."

They say a man ain't supposed to carry more than his share.

But nobody tells you what to do when life keeps handing you other people's load.

I didn't ask to be the example.

Didn't ask to be the one holding things together when everything around me was breaking apart.

But that's what happens when you're the big brother — you inherit the weight of what came before you.

My old man made a choice that split two homes in half.

Two women. Two sons. One last name.

One of us was raised in the light.

The other learned to love from the dark.

And somehow, it fell on me to hold us both up — even when he was the one pulling me down.

See, people talk about loyalty like it's a crown.

They forget it's heavy. It cuts. It costs.

And sometimes, the price ain't just your peace — it's your freedom.

I didn't plan to be my brother's keeper.

But life doesn't care what you plan.

It just puts the weight in your hands and dares you to carry it.

PREFACE
"When Blood Ain't Enough"

Every story I write carries a little truth.

Some truths come from what I've seen.

Others come from what I've survived.

My Brother's Keeper was born from the weight we inherit — the kind that doesn't show up on a scale but still bends your back.

Sometimes we carry our parents' mistakes, our lovers' pain, or our siblings' jealousy. We call it love. We call it loyalty. But really, it's survival dressed up as duty.

This story isn't about gang wars or prison time — it's about how choices ripple through bloodlines.

How one decision can turn peace into pride or pride into prison.

It's about what happens when two brothers grow up in the shadow of one man's secret, and how forgiveness becomes the only way out.

You can't help someone who won't help themselves.

But you can learn when to stop trying — and that's its own kind of freedom.

So, as you read this, remember:

Sometimes being your brother's keeper means letting go before you lose yourself.

by **Hayzel Greene**

TABLE OF CONTENTS

My Brother's Keeper

Hayzel Greene

Chapter One
The Pull-Up
Kid

There were fifty of us this year. We were flossed and polished, pulling up five rows deep, our jackets poppin', green and gold gleamin' in the sunlight. Deuce Boys representing.

All eyes were on us as we kicked our stands in unison, chrome glinting like a synchronized show. The smell of barbecue overpowered Lake Erie's funk; Speakers posted high on a flatbed truck, blasting EPMD's *'You Gots to Chill'*."

The annual MC picnic at Gordon Park was *that* event where every club, every rider, and every woman came to see and be seen. Booty shorts, Spandex, Gold hoops and glossed lips were everywhere. The ladies came out in all sides and shapes. Slim, slim-thick, thick and thick-thick were in attendance. Possibility was in the air.

All I had to say was someone was leaving here tonight with a new story. I rolled up solo, but that didn't mean I'd ride home alone. That was the best part of being single. Having freedom of choice without restraint and I planned to exercise it before the night was over.

"Yo, Kid, you flippin' a coin for it or what?"

"Maybe. Heads or tails, right?" I grinned. "Either way, I'm gettin' something or even both; some head and or some tail." I said licking my lips and rubbing my hands together in anticipation.

"You stupid for that one, Kid."

Laughter carried over the music, but my focus was already drifting across the park surveying the lay of the land. Then my whole mood shifted when I noticed Dice and his crew posted up under the big oak tree.

Dice and I had mad beef. We had been feuding for years. That nigga couldn't stand me, and the feeling was mutual. One would think it was because of money, or bikes, or even status. But nah, it was deeper than that. We'd been at odds since childhood, competing for respect that only one of us ever earned.

Today all beef was supposed to be left at the mouth of the drive. Today it was about brother and sisterhood. We came to ride, eat, and celebrate another year of loyalty and miles.

Still, I kept one eye on Dice. That's the kind of man he was smile in your face but always waiting for a chance to snake you.

It had been a long few months. I needed to be around my folks. To ride, check out some bikes, listen to some good music, and chill. Most of everything else was going to be a bonus. I need some R&R. The shop was finally back in the black after two slow seasons, and I'd been grindin' nonstop to keep my employees paid and my business alive.

My Pops used to tell me, *"A man's worth ain't in his bike, it's in how he handles the crash."*

And I'd had plenty of crashes, some metal and some emotional. So, when the picnic came around, it wasn't just another flex. It was a release. A reminder that I'd built something from the pavement up.

And maybe, just maybe, tonight I'd find someone who saw the man under the leather, someone who didn't just love the ride but understood the reason I kept my helmet on even when the engine stopped.

In the distance I heard bikes approaching. I turned towards the sound and saw ten females cruisin' up in perfect sequence, bikes accented in chocolate and pink. Once they stopped, they parked in formation. They kicked their stands, dismounted and heads turned like dominoes.

One beauty caught my eye. It was like the world slowed down as she took off her helmet.

My Brother's Keeper

Her hair flowed down her back in dark waves that brushed the top of her shoulders. Her hips curved like poetry, her confidence hit like a bass line. Her brown sun-kissed skin glowed, that kind of fine you don't recover from.

"Who is that?" I inquired.

"Hell, if I know," Spice said, already gawking. "Look at her girl. She's gorgeous."

"Y'all sittin' here actin' scared," Spud said, grinning. "I'm about to get names."

When he came back, he had the low down. "Maya is the short one," he pointed out, "Dezay is the other."

"Why haven't I ever seen her before, damn." I interjected. "What else did you find out?"

"If I can finish," he said.

I stared quietly waiting for him to give me the run down.

He cleared his throat, "Maya is from somewhere West and she came here to go to school."

"Good looking." I continued my stare while he told what he knew about the other female. Me, I was on a mission. We had plenty of women throwing looks our way, but Maya... I felt something different about her. That kind of energy that commanded my attention. And I was already hooked. I wanted to get to know a little bit more about her.

Hayzel Greene

Chapter Two
The New Girl
Maya

The air smelled like smoke, sweat, and barbecue. The kind of mix that clings to your clothes. The energy that made you feel alive. This is my first time hanging out with my cousin and her girls. It wasn't about attention, though. Maybe a little. I wanted to check out the scene and these fine ass men on their bikes.

We pulled into Gordon Park ten deep, our bikes humming low like a pack of wolves growling before the attack. The pink-and-chocolate jackets shimmered against the sun matching the accents on our bikes, *Chic Riders MC*. All eyes turned, just like we wanted.

I have been to Cleveland several times but never had I ever been out kicking it with my cousin and her crew. I was born and raised on the West Coast and only had been here for less than a month, so, I was still finding my rhythm. My cousin had been here her entire life, and she knew who was who, where to go and who not to trust.

Once it was official, I made sure to get a jacket like her and her girls since I was going to be joining the crew. It is a new city, new crew, same code: ride hard, stand tall, never let 'em see you sweat.

When I kicked my stand and pulled off my lid, I let my hair flow like I was in a Head and Shoulders commercial. I looked around and I could feel the heat from some stares. Now and days you do not know if people are looking at you because they want you, need you, or want to own you. But nine out of ten, they don't know what they want. Sometimes, neither do I, but looking at him. He had a look about himself. His energy gravitated towards me.

He leaned against his bike, green and gold leather, clean sneakers, confidence dripping like it was stitched into his jacket. He wasn't loud.

He didn't need to be. I think the ones who carry real weight don't need to be boisterous.

"Who is that?" I asked.

"Kid," another answered. "The president of the Deuce Boys'."

The chatter began. Stories of Kid's indiscretions: some bad and some messy. Someone said he had a temper, a past, a reputation for never backing down. But they also said he took care of his people. Something about that balance drew me in and had me curious. What I really wanted to know was whether he was really a bad boy?

Every time my eyes drifted in his direction, I caught him watching me. I looked away, slowly and measured I wasn't about to give myself away. But our eyes kept finding each other, lingering a little longer each time, turning into something unspoken and electric. A quiet game of cat and mouse, played in glances and pauses. I tried to call him to me without moving an inch, trusting the pull between us to do the work. He didn't rush it, didn't cross the space right away—and I appreciated that. I hated men who hurried the moment, even when my body was already leaning into the possibility of him.

My cousin's girls thought I came to Cleveland for bike life. The truth was, I came because I was accepted into CSU—and when my cousin opened her home to me, the decision became a no-brainer.

The West held too many ghosts. My love life was strained by an ex who couldn't handle my independence, a bike club that had turned political, and a city that no longer felt like home. Cleveland was supposed to be a reset.

So, I packed up my belongings—my bike included—and left. My intention was simple: ride under the radar, keep my distance, and focus on myself. I wasn't looking to be noticed, and I wasn't planning to start anything with any man anytime soon.

But when I saw him standing in that sea of chrome and color, he felt like a summons. His energy was thick, the kind you don't ignore even when you want to. I agreed to ride today with one plan—to pass through, make a few connections, and go home untouched. But the way he held my gaze told me I was already off course. I wouldn't be leaving the same way I came.

The Moment

The bass from the speakers thumped against my chest as I headed toward the concession stand. Then I caught it; the sexiest concoction brushing past me. I turned just as he approached.

My body went straight into fight-or-flight. I couldn't decide whether to divert him, turn on my heel, run, or stand my ground and fight the urge to press myself against him—take his scent with me so I could replay it later tonight. I stayed where I was, standing in line as the smell of him crept closer.

"You new out here?" he asked, his voice low and steady.

"That obvious?" I smiled, not turning around right away.

"Only to somebody who's been around long enough to recognize new energy."

When I finally faced him, he gave me that look—the kind that sees past what you're wearing and straight into what you're hiding.

"Maya," I said, extending my hand.

"Kid," he replied, taking it slow. His grip was firm, respectful. "Welcome to the city."

Right then, I knew this wasn't just another man trying to score—or was it? I couldn't tell if this was a pickup or the start of something with weight. He carried his name like both a badge and a burden. I'd heard things about Kid. The kind of man who could wreck me in all the right ways if I let him get too close.

Our gazes locked, my mind racing—and in that moment, I already knew.

I was in trouble.

Chapter Three
The Wait
Kid

What started as a ride here and there turned into something steady. It settled in slowly. Unspoken. One ride turned into another. And answered call without thinking. Time stacking quietly not putting a label on it at first, we just kept choosing each other while it felt natural.

One evening, we rode out just before dusk. No destination. No rush. The road stretched open in front of us, engines humming low, the sky bleeding into copper and gray. She rode beside me—not behind—and that mattered. We didn't say much. I didn't need to. The miles carried the conversation for us. When we finally pulled over, helmets off, the silence between us felt solid. Earned. That was when I knew this wasn't temporary.

We rode together. Laughed together. Slept tangled in the same sheets. But it wasn't just physical. There was something different about Maya.

Silence didn't feel empty around her. We'd lie there for hours, skin still warm, minds open, talking about dreams, fears, and the kinds of past mistakes we didn't usually name out loud. She didn't press or pry. She made space. Made it easy for me to be authentic—to simply be.

Despite how drawn I was to her; I didn't rush it. Every look from her pulled me in deeper, but patience came naturally. When it came time to make love to her, I wanted it to mean more than bodies aligned or a release. I wanted it to signify something. Intention. Choice.

We courted for months.

There were benefits to being a member of the Deuce Boys—but jealousy rode close behind. Some of the crew didn't like how much time I spent with her. They thought she was a distraction. What they didn't understand was that Maya wasn't just another pretty face from the ride circuit. She was peace in a world that rarely offered it.

One evening, she caught me off guard. Said that while we figured things out, it wouldn't bother her if I saw someone else.

Who does that?

What woman says she doesn't mind you dating other women while y'all figure things out?

It had to be a test—and I wasn't about to fail if it was. Some things are worth waiting for. So yeah, I played the long game. Every night she left me with thoughts I had to wrestle down. But when the time came, I already knew—she was going to have to earn what patience had built inside me.

Chapter Four
The Test
Maya

With Kid, time moved differently. Days slipped into long conversations, easy laughter, and late-night rides that made me forget I was supposed to be protecting my peace. He showed up in a way that was consistent, never aggressive, never performative. Just present.

Time he would pick me up in his car and we would just ride. Afterwards, we'd sit on the hood, watching streetlights flicker across the lake, and I'd feel a comfort I hadn't known for in a long time. I felt peace. He wasn't a rough biker who could throw fists. He was just him. Slow and attentive. He saw me without needing an explanation.

He never hurried me.

I never asked for more than I was willing to give. Never demanded more than I was ready to offer. That was what scared me the most. I'd been chased before, pursued by men who mistook urgency for interest. But Kid—he waited.

And every time he did, I wanted to give in.

So, I tested him.

I told him that until I was ready, he was free to do whatever he wanted— see whoever he wanted. He didn't argue. Didn't flinch. Just gave me that quiet, confident look that said, *I'll wait—but don't play if you don't mean it.*

I told myself it was a boundary. A way to keep him at a distance.

The truth was, I wanted to know if he was the kind of man who got distracted when patience was required.

He didn't.

And that changed everything.

Every time he walked away at the end of the night, my heart followed him halfway down the block. Every text, every laugh, every almost-kiss pulled me closer to something I couldn't quite name.

So yeah—I told him to take his time.

But deep down, I prayed he wouldn't.

Chapter Five
The Night She Chose Me
Kid

Every glance between us became more intense as the weeks stretched into months. The night the club reopened put a stop to whatever game we were playing, the testing, the waiting.

Everyone was excited about the completion of the reconstruction of the former Inner Circle on Lakeview. Fridays and Saturdays jumped, with couples wrapped over each other like satin, Deuce Boys were deep, music blaring, and money flowing.

Sweat and laughter pervaded the air by last call. The night was still humming in my chest when I finished my rounds, locked up, and walked out feeling terrific. Now all I wanted was sleep, quiet, and steam. Whichever came first.

The Shower

It was four a.m. by the time we made it to my house. I was desperate to feel the heat from the shower, the massage of the jets as they would hammer onto my taut muscles. As soon as the door closed behind us, I immediately stripped my way to the bathroom. My shoes scattered first, followed my shirt, leaving a trail of clothing in my wake.

Maya trailed behind, picking up clothes, fussing altering her tone between reprimand and amusement. "You know you pass the hamper on your way to the bathroom?"

"Sorry," I muttered. "I just need to wash today off me. So, I can cuddle next to you and rest my body." It was no time before the water hit the right temperature and I stepped in, closed my eyes, held myself up as I sank into the tile, inhaling into the silence as hot jets danced on my skin relieving today's tension.

I was so immersed that I didn't hear Maya enter the shower let alone the bathroom. The cool air announced her arrival as it brushed my back. The warmth of her body followed as her soft skin met mine.

She wrapped her arms around my waist bringing us closer. Her hug gave me a sense of assurance. I turned around and there she stood, watering her birthday suit. Her curls feel from the steam, her eyes calm like she'd been thinking about this longer than I had. Whatever fatigue I had left dissolved right there.

Water ran over her shoulders, tracing every curve like it had been waiting. The closer she got, the heat between my thighs had my rise. Her hand slid up my chest, fingers spreading over the tattoo near my heart. I could see in her face that she was ready.

For a moment we just stood there, forehead to forehead, breathing the same air. The sound of the water softened into rhythm steady, pulsing. Then she kissed me. Slow, deep, like she was testing my resolve.

Everything after that was muscle memory. I lifted her inserting me inside of her as our lips sensually pecked until she fully opened her mouth to receive my tongue.

I lost it when she moaned into my mouth letting me know that she felt our energy surging. I slowly moved myself in and out of her as her legs crossed my lower back. Her inner walls clinched and released as I rocked. She buried her face within my neck peppering kisses sensually.

Her body fits against mine in a way that makes time irrelevant. Her pheromones cooked in my nostrils as the steam filled the shower walls. My legs felt weak, and I had no clue how I was going to hold our weight. I was reaching my peak but wanted her to reach hers first. I slowed my pace whispered in her ear how good she felt on my dick.

I needed the release but not before she did. When I felt my surge approaching, I pulled back, breaking our embrace and putting her back on her feet. "Let's go." I spoke.

My Brother's Keeper

The Shift

Our bodies were still wet from the rain of the shower heads when I guided us to the bedroom. Barely making it to the bed, I slowly kissed her damp body as I positioned in the center of the bed, staring with her eyelids, down the bridge of her nose, our lips finally nestling on each other until I breathed her in.

She motioned me to let her take control mounting me as she continued peppering me with kisses. Her mouth moved lower, soft trails of heat over my chest, my stomach. By the time she reached the inside of my thighs, I was gone.

Her tongue circled me like she was learning a song only she could play. Every lick, every pull of her lips drew a sound from me I didn't know I could make. When she took me deeper, rhythm matching the rain of shower together still hitting the bathroom tile, and I couldn't do anything but surrender.

I warned her I was close. She hummed in satisfaction. Surprising me, she got up and sat comfortably on my thighs, positioning herself to take me inside her heat. She slid down on me slowly, picking up her pace as she bounced up and down repeatedly teasing my desire to release.

The Ride

Inch by inch, breath catching, body tightening around me until we both groaned. It wasn't just sex; it was longing from the weeks of restraint unraveling in every roll of her hips. Her movements were steady, deliberate, like she knew exactly how to drive me to the edge and keep me there. I was her puppet, and she was my puppeteer. I gripped her waist assisting her ride, guiding, meeting her rhythm until the world narrowed to heat and heartbeat.

Her walls started to constrict around me. Her pace picked up, her moans turned into pants and her pants turned into chants. She was coming to an understanding that our bodies were in agreeance. Watching her when we came, it wasn't rushed or wild, it was timed, it was full. A crash we'd both seen coming. But for some reason it was still a surprise. She collapsed against my chest, trembling. I wrapped my arms around her, too spent to speak, too alive to sleep.

For the first time in a long time, I wasn't thinking about tomorrow. Just her heartbeat against mine and the quiet truth that patience had been worth every damn minute.

Chapter Six
The Calm
Maya

The night felt endless. Time lost its shape, replaced by the rhythm of our breathing, the warmth of skin against skin, and the quiet understanding our bodies had already reached long before we did.

I tried to hold on to control—to take it slow, to protect what little peace I had left. But the moment I saw him standing in that shower, water tracing over his back, strength softened by exhaustion, I knew it was already over. I'd waited long enough. Waiting had become its own kind of ache.

And I was done denying it.

When I stepped into him, the hunger in his eyes spoke louder than words ever could. Every touch, every kiss, every sound that slipped from me wasn't just want—it was release. For months, I'd lived in the space between wanting him and needing him. That space disappeared the second he pulled me close.

He held me like he understood what this cost me. Like he knew this wasn't just about my body, it was about trust finally catching up to desire. About letting go of the rules I'd built to keep myself untouched.

After, I lay against his chest and listened to his heartbeat—slow, steady, grounding. Outside, the city was quiet. Inside that room, I felt awake in a way I hadn't in years.

He drifted into sleep with his arm heavy around me. I stayed awake a little longer, memorizing the rise and fall of his breathing, the shape of his face in the dark. I wanted to remember that peace. The stillness. The way everything felt right for once.

Because something deep in my gut told me this was the calm before the chaos.

And those nights like this don't last as long as you want them to.

Chapter Seven
Dice Rolled
Kid

Circle Night always landed loud, lit, and loyal. Every frequent rider knew the drill. We packed into Da Dub Shack—the Deuce Boys' spot—where Saturday nights felt more like religion than routine.

DJ Corkscrew had the tables blazing. Old-school hip-hop cut through the crowd—*Paul Revere, Eric B. for President*. The bass rattled the floor, shots passed from hand to hand, and familiar laughter bounced off the walls.

I kept it light. One or two drinks. Just enough to be social. I never liked getting sloppy while working. A man had to stay alert. All it took was one drunk fool testing the wrong person and the whole night could go left.

Right on cue, Dice walked in with his boys.

The room didn't stop—but it shifted. Subtle. The kind of change most people miss. I felt it anyway, heat crawling up my neck.

We hadn't exchanged words in months, but the air between us stayed sour. Still, I nodded his way, keeping it respectful. He nodded back, jaw tight.

For a second, I thought maybe we'd make it through the night without bullshit.

I was wrong.

Maya slipped her arms around my waist from behind, grounding me before the tension could take over. Standing five-five, soft but solid, she had a way of pulling me back without saying a word. Her warmth cooled the heat Dice brought in with him.

"You good?" she whispered.

"Yeah," I said, jaw still tight. "I'm good now."

Then the music cut.

Blue lights flashed. Cleveland PD stormed in like they were raiding a cartel.

"Hands where we can see 'em! IDs out—now!"

The room froze. Bottles clinked. A few people tried to melt into the background, but it was already too late. Cops moved fast, barking orders, running names.

I wasn't worried. I hadn't done shit.

When the officer called my name, I stayed calm.

Then I heard it.

"Warrant hit—Andre Johnson. Step forward."

My stomach dropped.

"Warrant?" I spat. "That's a mistake."

They didn't care. Hands behind my back. Cuffs tight. Maya's voice cut through the noise.

"Wait—what's going on? He didn't do anything!"

I tried to speak, but they weren't listening.

I'd never been in trouble. Not once.

This had Dice written all over it.

That bitch-ass nigga.

I should've known better than to let him back in my orbit. Pops always preached loyalty—*look out for your brother*. I did. Pops didn't know Dice the way I did.

My Brother's Keeper

We didn't share a mother—just a house. That's where the competition started. He was twelve when he came to live with us. I was already fourteen, old enough to understand why he looked at me like I was the reason his life changed.

He never let that go.

My moms still took him in. Fed him. Loved him like her own.

So, I did too. Rode for him. Backed him.

And this was how he paid me back.

All his life, Dice tried to one-up me. Never could.

I learned early that muscle only takes you so far. A man's real power is how he thinks. I was the bookworm. I graduated early. Built something real. Built the Deuce Boys from the ground up.

And now, because of him, I was being dragged out of my own club in cuffs like a criminal in a place I built.

Hayzel Greene

Chapter Eight
When the Music Stopped
Maya

One second the bass was shaking the walls, and the next, it vanished. Not faded. Gone. The kind of silence that hits before you understand something has gone wrong.

Blue lights hit the windows, and officers poured into the club like a wave. Yelling, pushing, barking orders. I froze for half a second, trying to process what was happening. Then I saw Kid's hands in the air and my heart jumped into my throat.

"Everyone show ID! Nobody moves!"

I fumbled for my wallet, pulse thudding in my ears. Around me, people were arguing, some trying to slide out the back. But Kid stood still— calm, collected, like he'd already been through this before.

He hadn't.

When they called his name, *Andre Johnson*—I almost laughed, thinking it had to be a mistake. But the officer didn't hesitate. Cuffed him fast, even as officers moved through the club, pulling others from both crews toward the door.

"Wait! That's not right—he doesn't even have a record!" I shouted, stepping forward.

One of the cops pushed me back, hard enough to make me stumble. I could see the confusion on Kid's face turning into frustration. He tried to reason with them, voice low but sharp. They weren't listening. They'd already decided who he was.

The whole time, Dice stood a few feet away, already restrained, watching it all unfold without a flicker of emotion. No emotion. Just… watching. My stomach twisted.

It hit me right then—this wasn't random.

They marched Kid through the crowd along with several others, but he was the only one I could see. People whispered, shook their heads, and took out phones to record. My chest burned. He looked over his shoulder once—just once—and that look said everything: Don't *make this worse. Stay calm. I'll handle it.*

I nodded even though my eyes stung.

I wanted to run after him, grab his arm, explain for him, something, anything, but the cops shoved him into the back of a squad car and slammed the door.

The lights spun against his face as they pulled off, and in that reflection, I saw everything we'd built start to unravel.

Dice was still standing there when I turned around. That same smug grin he wore at Gordon Park creeping up again. And that's when it clicked.

The warrant. The timing. The setup. He did this.

He saw something in Kid he couldn't match—a man who didn't need to prove he was one.
And instead of facing that truth, he tried to break it.

I walked past him slow, close enough for him to hear me whisper, "You might've set him up, but this ain't over."

He didn't respond, just smirked and turned away.

That night, I couldn't sleep. Kid's scent was still on the sheets; his jacket still draped over the chair. I kept replaying the sound of those cuffs clicking shut, the way he looked back at me one last time.

I promised myself I'd be there for him—whatever came next. He waited for me when he didn't have to. Now it was my turn to wait for him.

Chapter Nine
Detained
Kid

They gave me a moment with Maya before transport.

"Maya, call my mother," I said quietly. "Tell her what happened—and where I'll be."

She nodded, trying to stay steady, eyes shining anyway.

I turned to the officer. "Can I give her my keys and my belongings?"

He hesitated, then nodded once.

I handed Maya my wallet, my chain, my watch—kept two hundred in my pocket. She held everything like it mattered, like if she dropped any of it, I might disappear too. I wanted to pull her close, tell her it would be alright, but the cuffs were already biting into my wrists. Comfort wasn't something I could offer like that.

Ten of us got hauled off that night—me, Dice, and eight others.

I could understand half of them being there. They stayed in trouble, lived close to the edge. But me? I was built different. I worked too hard, thought too far ahead, to end up behind bars over something that wasn't even mine.

The ride downtown was quiet. Nobody had much to say once the doors closed. Just the rattle of chains and the low hum of the engine carrying us where we didn't want to go.

Processing blurred together after that—fingerprints pressed into cold glass, a camera flashing for a mug shot, officers looking through me like I was just another number. Shoes squeaked on waxed floors. Chains clinked every time someone shifted. Men pretended they weren't scared.

All I could think about was how I'd rather be anywhere else.

If I was being honest, I'd rather have been home searching Maya, tangled up in her, instead of standing naked in front of strangers telling me to turn and cough. To keep myself from snapping, I replayed her in my head.

Her laugh. That crease in her smile when she teased me. The way she walked away slowly on purpose, just to make me look.

Remembering her was the only thing that kept me steady.

By the time they locked us into holding, it was clear we weren't going anywhere fast. The warrant flagged on my name meant I had to wait it out. Courts don't move on weekends, and nobody cared that the mistake wasn't mine—not yet.

They kept us locked up the whole weekend waiting for a court date.

Time moved like molasses. Slow. Sticky. Heavy.

A few of my boys from the set were there, which helped. We stuck together, kept our heads down, stayed sharp. I knew they had my back the same way I'd always had theirs.

Dice, though—I didn't trust him as far as I could throw him.

If anything went down, he'd be the first to point a finger, the first to save himself. I'd spent my whole life watching him do just enough damage to stay standing while someone else paid the price.

I lay on that hard cot staring at the ceiling, counting cracks, thinking about how one wrong letter—a missing "z" in a damn name—was about to cost me everything I'd built.

And all I could do was wait.

Chapter Ten
The Wait
Maya

The first night he was gone, the house felt too still. His cologne lingered in the air; his jacket draped over the chair like he'd only stepped outside for a smoke.

I kept expecting to hear the rumble of his bike, the jingle of his keys — something that said he was on his way home.

But silence answered back every time.

I tried to sleep, but my mind kept replaying the sound of those handcuffs, the flash of red and blue lights bouncing across his face. I could still hear his voice telling me to call his mother, to let her know what happened. The way he said it — calm, steady, even with the cops gripping his arms — told me he already knew he wasn't coming home that night.

I called the county jail first thing that morning, my voice sharp from no sleep. They gave me nothing but rules and runarounds. "Can't release information until booking's complete." "Try back later." "Ma'am, we can't confirm who's in custody without a case number." That's when I understood—until he was fully processed, he was just another name in the system.

By the fifth call, I stopped asking politely.

Then I called his mother. She answered on the first ring, voice shaking but strong. "I already know, baby. Maya, thank you for calling me."

We sat on the phone in silence for a moment — two women connected by worry for the same man.

Day turned to night, night back to day. I kept busy staying sane, rode with my girls, helped out at the shop, anything to keep from breaking down. But every time my phone buzzed, I stopped breathing for a second, hoping it was him.

Word spread quickly. Some people talked like they knew the whole story. Others whispered like I was supposed to be embarrassed for standing by him. I didn't care. Half those people had never known what it felt like to love somebody solid.

Dice's name came up more than once. I ignored it the first few times, but deep down, I knew. He'd been too quiet. Too clean. Too smug when the cops showed up.

By the weekend, I was done crying. I sat at the kitchen table with a notepad and pen, writing down everything I wanted to say when he could finally hear me again.

If they thought they could break him, they didn't know the kind of man he was. And if they thought I was gonna disappear just because it got hard — they didn't know me either.

I promised myself I'd be there when he called. I'd write. I'd visit. I'd wait.

Because love doesn't vanish when the door locks it learns how to survive the echo.

Chapter Eleven
The Sentence
Kid

The courtroom smelled like dust and cheap perfume. I sat there cuffed, shoulders straight, eyes forward, trying to hold on to a little pride even though the odds were stacked against me. Maya was in the back, right behind my mother — both of them quiet, both of them praying with their eyes open.

The judge barely looked up when she said my name. "**Andre Johnson**," she read, flipping through a file like I was a number instead of a person. "Probation violation tied to a theft charge. Two years in state custody."

Two years.

My stomach dropped.

I wanted to laugh because it sounded ridiculous.

I had never even been in trouble — not a ticket, not a warning. The system didn't care about that. All they knew was that **Andre Johnson** matched their paperwork.

They didn't care that **Andrez Johnson** — my brother — was the real one they wanted.

I spoke up anyway. "Your Honor, I think you have the wrong person." She looked at me like she'd heard that line a thousand times. "Mr. Johnson, your record speaks for itself."

That's when I knew it didn't matter what I said. In this room, truth didn't make a sound.

It hit me sitting there in that stiff wooden chair. He did this on purpose. Dice. Left out the "z" in his name like it was nothing. Like my life didn't mean shit. It didn't help that our birthdays were the same damn day —

two years apart — or that we'd always been tied together whether we wanted to be or not.

He'd found a way to make sure I carried his mess again. Typical.

And there was nothing I could do but watch that gavel come down and seal it.

When they escorted me out, I didn't look back. Couldn't. If I turned around and saw the pain in my mother's eyes or the tears building in Maya's, I would've lost it.

So, I kept my head high, jaw locked, walking through those doors like a man who wasn't broken — even if I was.

They say time starts when the bars close behind you. But for me, it started the moment I realized blood doesn't always make you family.

Chapter Twelve
The Inside
Kid

The first week felt like a month. Same gray walls. Same metal trays. Same echoes bouncing off the tier. You learn the rhythm quick in here—when the lights snap on, when they kill the noise, when to move, when to blend. You keep your head down and your fists ready, just in case.

Mail Call was the only thing that broke the monotony.

"Andre Johnson… Andre Johnson… Andre Johnson."

Every time they called my name, heads turned. Felt like I was the most popular man in the joint. Maya's letters came one after another—tight cursive, perfume faint enough to cut through steel and bleach. I'd fold them, tuck them in my pocket, and wait until lights-out to read. In a place where everything is hard and cold, her words were soft and warm. They reminded me of what home sounded like.

Some of the guys called me lucky. Others were just thirsty for a glimpse of the paper. Mail was gold in here; men would trade cigarettes just to feel connected to somebody. I kept mine close. Nobody was touching that piece of peace.

Afternoons, the yard became our therapy. Me and my crew—Spud, Rico, and Twin—posted near the weight benches. I stayed pushing iron, keeping my body sharp. Two-fifty solid, six-pack tight, arms cut deep enough to make the COs stare. They couldn't figure out how somebody my size could move that much weight, but discipline doesn't need to brag. It shows.

Most days stayed quiet, until Dice found a way to mess that up.

He'd been running his mouth again, trying to claim something—or somebody—that was already spoken for. Typical. Some things never changed, even behind bars. I saw the group gathering across the yard. Trevor and his boys closing in on Dice, faces set like it was about to get ugly.

For a minute, I just watched. I tried to let it play out. But when that first punch landed, instinct took over.

I stood, nodded to Spud, and crossed the yard. By the time I got there, Trevor was shouting, "Who the fuck you think you are, claimin' my bitch?"

Dice looked rattled, mouth twitching, eyes darting my way. I should've left him to it. But Pops raised me better than that. Even if he was the reason I was locked up, he was still blood.

"I think you need to claim another one," I said, stepping between them. "Because this one ain't yours." "Who the fuck is you?" Trevor barked. "Don't worry about it. Just know this man ain't gonna be your bitch."

I turned to Dice.

"You wanna be his bitch?" "Hell naw," he shot back, shaking his head hard. "Then it's settled," I said. "If he's anybody's bitch, he's mine."

Laughter rippled through the crowd—half shock, half respect. Then Trevor's boy lunged.

Spud caught him with an uppercut so clean it echoed. Another swung at me; I slipped it, came back with a gut shot and a right that dropped him cold. After that, it was chaos—fists, boots, curses. Dice finally jumped in, and for the first time in our lives, we were fighting on the same side.

Guards rushed in swinging billy clubs, sirens screaming. It didn't matter who started it; we were all going down.

My Brother's Keeper

They threw us in segregation—concrete box, one dim light, silence thick enough to choke on. Time slows different in the hole. No clocks, no windows, just your own thoughts playing back on repeat.

I sat there fuming, knuckles bruised, body aching, thinking about how every bad turn in my life somehow had Dice's fingerprints on it. And still—I'd jumped in for him. Because somewhere deep down, I couldn't stand to see him broken.

That's the curse of being your brother's keeper. You save him, even when he's the one drowning you.

Hayzel Greene

Chapter Thirteen
Letters inside the hole
Kid

It dawned on me that I still had Maya's letter tucked inside my sock. I pulled it out carefully, smoothing the creases, and leaned back against the wall to read.

Hey My Somebody,

I miss you.

I stopped by to see your folks. They're holding it together worried, but good. They ask about you like you're just out on a long ride and not somewhere they can't reach.

I know it's only been a little over a week, but I already miss your presence. The way you'd pull me close at night, how safe it felt lying against you until sleep took over.

I keep replaying our first night together. The way you took your time with me. The way you made me forget everything outside that room. Just thinking about it still makes my body respond to you.

When you read this, breathe me in. I pressed a little of my perfume into the paper so you won't forget my scent. I want you to remember how I sound when I want you, how my body reacts to yours.

I can't wait until you come home so I can remind you in person.

Until then, keep me close.

Remember that bay! I miss the shit out of you. I can't wait until you get home so I can see you. Here is a picture of what I am like when I think of you. I drip for you.

Have a good night…next letter with more.

Love You! Maya

I closed my eyes and let her words settle into me.

Even in the hole, surrounded by concrete, silence, and my own thoughts, she still found a way to reach me. Her letter wasn't just paper. It was air. It reminded me I was still somebody's man, not just another number stamped on a jumpsuit.

I read it again, slower this time. Every line pulled me back to the parts of us that felt untouched by this place—the laughter, the quiet moments, the way she looked at me like I was more than what the system said I was.

When the lights cut off, I folded the letter carefully and pressed it to my chest. In the dark, I could hear her voice, feel her presence, let it steady my breathing.

Three meals a day. Five minutes of peace each time. That's what life boiled down to in here.

I stopped counting days. Started counting reasons to get out.

Maya was reason one.

Chapter Fourteen
Freedom to Population
Kid

Finally—I was back.

My celly filled me in on what I'd missed. Trevor's boys tried to corner the cigarette market and got handled for it. Some dudes never learn. Just because one of them tested me before didn't mean I forgot. I made sure he remembered who he was dealing with.

The air felt different out here. Still foul, still heavy—but it smelled like movement. Like purpose.

I found Dice on the tier later that day. We came out of the hole together, both quiet, both worn down.

We finally talked.

He admitted what I already knew—that he'd been bitter, jealous, angry about being left behind. Said he'd been carrying it since he was twelve. I listened. Then I told him the truth.

He didn't have to hate me for what I had. My moms loved him like her own, even when he made it hard. He'd been so busy gripping the past he never noticed that part.

Then I laid it out straight.

"If anybody should've been mad, it should've been me. Your mama knew my mom existed and still tried to break up her home. She failed. And my mom took you in anyway. So, stop punishing me for something she did."

Something cracked in him. The anger drained from his face.

That was as close to peace as we were ever gonna get.

After that, I focused on what came next. I had a plan—and this time, I was the one running the game.

You learn quickly here that everything sells. Cigarettes. Candy. Information. But nothing moves faster than fantasy. Men in cages will pay for escape, and nothing offers escape like a letter.

Maya's letters kept me sane in the hole. I knew exactly what that kind of paper could do.

So, I wrote to her. Told her to round up a few of her girls—have them write letters, take pictures. Sweet, bold, whatever would sell. People trusted Maya. She had that way about her.

I told her to tap her cousin too, the one running with a different crowd. If we were doing this, we'd cover every taste.

Within a week, an envelope showed up thick with opportunity. Ten letters from women. Six from men. Each one paired with a photo.

I priced them by promise—the look, the story, the illusion of connection. By the end of the week, every single one was gone.

Business was booming.

Even Dice couldn't hide his envy watching my canteen stack up. Still, I broke him off—snacks, smokes. Enough to remind him we were square.

It's in my nature to share the win. That's what leaders do.

Two nights and a wake-up left.

After two years of concrete and noise, I could almost taste fresh air. Before I left, I passed the hustle down to my celly—told him I'd keep supply moving from the outside. Everybody eats when the system is tight.

Out of the original crew, I was the last one standing. Still here. Still focused. Still innocent—even after being proven guilty.

Freedom was coming.

My Brother's Keeper

And this time, I wasn't leaving empty-handed.

Hayzel Greene

Chapter Fifteen
The Return
Kid

I walked angry with two hundred fifty dollars and a head full of plans —
but I left that gate with more than I came in with. A mini empire. A
brother who finally saw me for who I was. And a woman who never
stopped believing I'd make it home.

Maya was waiting by the car, arms open, eyes already full of everything I
didn't have to say. The moment she touched me, the noise in my head
went quiet. Her warmth hit me first — soft, certain, like peace finally had
a body. I bent down, kissed her forehead, and for the first time in
months, I was able to breathe without the weight.

By the time we made it home, I was peeling out of those same clothes
that smelled like metal and dust. Freedom had its own scent — soap,
candles, something sweet burning low. I could hear the bathwater
running, the quiet hum of R&B under her breath as she moved around
the room.

The bathroom lights were low, steam already rising. She'd lit my favorite
scent, *Pi Type,* a smell that used to follow me through every late night at
the club. The air was warm, thick with comfort.

I sank into the tub, water wrapping around me like relief. Every ache in
my body let go at once. I didn't even hear her at first — the sound of her
steps soft against the tile. When I lifted the towel from my eyes, she was
there, standing close enough for me to see her reflection in the water.

No words. Just a look.

Maya reached for my hand and slid it up her thigh until it met bare skin.
Her breath caught, quiet but sure.

"You home now," she whispered. "Let me remind you what that feels like."

The air between us changed — not rushed, not hungry, just heavy with everything we'd both carried. Her skin was warm; the scent of her lotion mixed with the steam. When she knelt beside the tub, I could see the reflection of light sliding across her collarbone, the way her fingers brushed water against my chest, tracing slow circles.

Every touch felt like something being restored — not lust but belonging. The kind of love that doesn't need to prove itself, only exists.

When I stood, she rose with me. Her hands moved to my shoulders, steady, guiding, her eyes asking permission she already had. I pulled her close, skin to skin, the warmth of her body meeting mine like a promise.

We didn't rush it. Didn't chase the moment. We just *remembered each other.*

Her sigh became my breath. Her heartbeat found mine. And when we moved together, it wasn't about release — it was about return.

That night, the world outside didn't exist. Just her, the scent of Pi in the air, and the sound of water spilling over the edge of the tub — the kind of peace you don't get twice in a lifetime.

When we finally stepped out of the tub, the air felt different—warmer somehow, charged but calm. She handed me a towel and started drying me off like she was memorizing every inch of skin she'd missed while I was gone. Her touch was deliberate, steady. No rush.

I caught her hand midway, pulled her close until her chest rested against mine.

"I missed this," I whispered. "I know," she said, looking up at me. "But you're here now. So, stay."

Those words hit harder than I expected. *Stay.* After everything I'd been through—bars, fights, silence—that one word felt like a prayer.

My Brother's Keeper

We moved to the bedroom, the lights dim, sheets clean and soft. The scent of the candle followed us—vanilla and wood smoke blending with the faint musk of freedom. I sat on the edge of the bed, watching her. Not as a man starving for what he lost, but as one who couldn't believe it was finally real again.

She climbed into my lap, knees on either side, her forehead resting against mine. For a moment, neither of us moved. I could feel her heartbeat, quick but steady, syncing with mine. Her fingers traced the line of my jaw, down the back of my neck, settling over the tattoo on my shoulder like she was reminding herself where I'd come from.

"You feel different," she murmured.

"Maybe I am."

"Nah," she smiled faintly. "You just tired of carrying everything."

She was right.

So, I let it all go—every fight, every cold night, every word I never said.

When I kissed her, it wasn't fire. It was release. The kind that starts in your chest and spills out slowly. Our movements were unhurried, deliberate. She pressed her palms to my chest like she was grounding me, and I held her hips as if I was afraid to let go again.

Each breath between us said what words couldn't. Each touch felt like a piece of home being rebuilt.

The world outside our walls didn't exist—just the rhythm of us finding each other again. No walls, no time, no noise. Only her voice against my ear whispering my name like forgiveness.

When we finally lay back, skin damp and hearts steady, she rested her head on my chest. My hand found her back, tracing slow lines until her breathing evened out.

For the first time in a long time, I didn't feel like I owed anybody anything. Not the streets. Not the crew. Not even redemption.

Just this moment. Just her.

Peace didn't come loud—it came soft. And that night, it came in the form of her sleeping against me while the candle burned down to nothing.

Chapter Sixteen
What Home Feels Like
Maya/Kid

Maya

The morning, he was due out, I woke before the alarm. Couldn't eat. Couldn't sit still. The house felt too clean, too quiet—like it was holding its breath right along with me.

I'd washed the sheets twice, cooked enough food for a family, and still found something else to wipe down. When you've waited two years for someone you love, every detail starts to feel like a prayer.

The scent of *Taylor Made's Pi Type by Givenchy* filled the air. I lit it early so the house would smell like home by the time he walked through the door. That scent always reminded me of him—warm, confident, a little dangerous.

When the phone buzzed and I heard, *"I'm out,"* my knees almost gave out.
I didn't even realize I was crying until I tasted the salt.

When the lock of the last gate clanked, seeing him step out under open sky, something loose inside me. He looked different—still him, but heavier on the shoulders, quieter in the eyes. Two years behind walls will do that.

When he spotted me, he smiled slowly, like he had to remember how. And then he was in front of me, sunlight on his face, arms open. All that waiting, all that worry—gone in one breath.

For a long moment we just held on. No words, no explanations, just heartbeat against heartbeat. That was enough.

Once we reached the house, he barely made it through the door before he started stripping out of those prison-issue clothes. I laughed, half from joy, half from disbelief that he was really here. I ran his bath, poured in the oil, and turned down the lights.

Steam curled through the room, carrying the scent of Pi. When he finally eased into the water, eyes closed, I watched him exhale years of tension. The man who'd gone in angry and betrayed was finally free—not just in body, but in spirit.

I wanted to touch him, but I didn't. Not yet. This moment wasn't about desire; it was about peace. Letting the silence say what words couldn't.

He lifted the towel from his eyes and looked at me, smiling for real this time. And just like that, everything was right again.

Kid

I got home around four, stripped on my way to the bathroom, leaving a trail of clothes behind me. Maya followed, fussing about me dropping everything, her voice half-laugh, half-lecture.

"You can't even make it to the hamper?" she said, scooping up my shirt. "Later," I mumbled, already walking. "Just need that water."

The only thing I wanted was heat—something steady and clean to wash the day off me. Hot jets pounded against tense muscles; I leaned into the tile, eyes closed, breathing through the quiet. The kind of silence that hums right before you fall asleep.

I didn't hear her at first, the faint click of the door, the cool air brushing my back. Then came warmth—soft skin meeting mine, slow and sure. When I turned, she was there. Naked. Hair damp from the steam, eyes calm like she'd been thinking about this longer than I had.

Whatever fatigue I had left dissolved right there.

Water ran over her shoulders, tracing every curve like it had been waiting its turn. She stepped closer, the heat between us rising until the air itself felt alive. Her hand slid up my chest, fingers spreading over the tattoo near my heart. I could see it in her face—this wasn't about lust; it was about confirmation. About reminding us both that we'd made it through.

For a moment we just stood there, forehead to forehead, breathing the same air. The sound of the water softened into rhythm—steady, pulsing.

Then she kissed me. Slow, deep, like she was testing to make sure I was real.

Everything that came after moved like memory—natural, unhurried. Her body fit against mine in a way that made time irrelevant. The scent of her mixed with the soap and steam, and for a second, I forgot where one of us ended and the other began.

When she finally pulled back, her voice was low but certain.

"You home now," she whispered.

I nodded, hands on her waist, grounding myself in that truth. No walls, no noise, no weight. Just her, warm and close, the water washing over us both—like it was baptizing what was broken.

When we finally stepped out, the mirror was fogged, the whole room wrapped in heat. She handed me a towel and started drying me off— slow, careful—like she was relearning the shape of me. Every pass of her hand said, *"I missed you.*

I caught her wrist and pulled her close. Her skin was still warm from the water, and when her body met mine, the rest of the world just... disappeared.

"You sure about this?" I asked, my voice low. "I've been sure," she whispered. "I just needed you home to prove it."

That was all it took.

We moved to the bedroom, the scent of steam and *Pi Type* trailing behind us. The sheets were cool, soft against skin that was anything but. She climbed into bed first, pulling me with her, her hands finding their way like they'd been counting the days.

No rush. No edge. Just patience—the kind that comes from missing somebody so long you forget what it feels like to touch them.

Her fingers traced the scars across my shoulder, pausing over one like she could erase it. I caught her hand and kissed her palm.

"Don't," I said softly. "They're part of the story."

She nodded, eyes locked on mine, then pressed her lips to the same spot.

The room was quiet except for our breathing and the slow creak of the mattress as we met in the middle—steady, certain. Every touch was deliberate, every breath synced. This wasn't about catching up; it was about *reclaiming time.*

When I pulled her closer, she wrapped her legs around me, grounding me to the moment. Her whisper came soft against my ear:

"Don't go nowhere."

"I ain't," I breathed. "Not ever again."

We moved together—two people who'd been through hell and finally found their way back to themselves.

When it was over, she laid her head on my chest, her hand resting right over my heart. I could feel her heartbeat matching mine—slow, steady, home.

I kissed the top of her head and exhaled. For the first time in years, I wasn't running from anything. Not guilt. Not anger. Not even the past.

Just lying there—skin to skin, breath to breath—I realized peace didn't come easy. But right then, in that moment, it finally felt possible.

Maya

My Brother's Keeper

That night, after he fell asleep, I just lay there watching him breathe. The rhythm was steady, sure—the kind you forget you ever lived without.

I traced the outline of his hand resting on my thigh and thought about all the nights I'd reached across cold sheets hoping he'd still come home. Two years of writing letters, talking to walls, praying to a God I wasn't sure was still listening—all so I could feel this moment.

He looked peaceful, almost boyish in sleep. The lines around his mouth softened, the tension in his jaw gone. I wanted to memorize this quiet version of him, unguarded, unburdened. The man I loved, not the man the world tried to turn him into.

The candle burned low, the scent of *Pi* still hanging in the air. It mixed with the smell of his skin, and I swear, if love had a fragrance, that was it—patience and warmth with a hint of smoke.

I thought about everything he'd carried—the weight of his father's mistakes, the shadow of his brother, the way loyalty can sometimes feel like punishment. He called it survival. I called it endurance.

But tonight wasn't about what we'd lost. It was about what we still had.

He murmured something in his sleep, my name maybe, and reached for me without opening his eyes. His hand found my hip like it belonged there.

That's when I knew—no matter what came next, no matter how hard peace would be to keep—this was our reset. Not the end of the storm, but the first clear morning after it.

And I wasn't letting go.

Hayzel Greene

Chapter Seventeen
The Cookout
Kid

The Weight of Blood

Morning came soft through the blinds, thin strips of light cutting across the sheets.

Maya was still asleep beside me, her hand on my chest, her breathing calm. The house was quiet—too quiet, almost—but not in that heavy way. It was the kind of quiet you earn.

I slipped out of bed, pulled on sweats, and stood at the window for a while. The neighborhood looked the same, but I didn't. Two years will do that to a man. It makes you see peace as a privilege, not a promise.

The smell of coffee drifted down the hall—rich, familiar. Pops was already up. He'd always been that way, sun barely up and his thoughts already halfway through the day.

I followed the smell of coffee into the kitchen. Pops was already at the table, newspaper folded but unread, his mug untouched like he'd been thinking longer than he'd been sipping.

"You up early," he said without looking up. "Guess I ain't used to real beds yet." "That'll change," he murmured, finally meeting my eyes. "Everything changes when you start living again."

He motioned for me to sit. I did, leaning forward, elbows on the table.

"How it feel?" he asked.

"Different," I said. "Good different, but... still trying to breathe normal, you know?"

He nodded, quiet for a moment.

"You always carried the world on your back, son. Even when you was little. Tried to fix what wasn't yours to fix."

I didn't say anything. He was right.

"Dice came by last week," Pops went on. "Brought Nicole. Said he was gonna do better."
"Yeah. We talked a little. I think he mean it this time."
"I think he do too. But I also think y'all got more healing to do than you think."

I rubbed my jaw, watching the way his hand circled his mug but never lifted it.

"You did right by him in there," Pops said softly. "That wasn't no small thing. But I don't want you to carry that man's choices for the rest of your life. You hear me?"
"Yeah."
"No," he said, leaning forward. "I mean really hear me."

His eyes were steady, firm but kind.

"Being your brother's keeper don't mean losing yourself in the process. It means knowing when to pull him up, but also when to let him stand on his own."

I sat back, the weight of his words sitting heavy but right.

"So, what I'm supposed to do, Pops?" I asked quietly.

"You are supposed to live, son. And keep living. Don't let guilt turn into purpose. Let love do that."

He gave a small smile, the kind that meant the conversation was done—but the message wasn't.

By the time the afternoon settled in, the house felt fuller. Moms and Pops had turned my first day home into something familiar—charcoal smoke in the air, music drifting through the yard, voices folding over each other like they used to.

My Brother's Keeper

The smell of charcoal and hickory hit me before I even stepped into the yard. Laughter floated through the air, mixed with the sound of old-school R&B and the clink of soda bottles against the cooler.

Spud and Spice were there with their girls, already talking trash over dominoes. Dice showed up too, Nicole on his arm. Funny how life cycles back, Maya's girl was the one who'd written him letters while we were down, and now they were standing side by side like something new had started between them.

When I walked in, Dice stood up and nodded. For a moment, the whole yard went quiet.
Then Moms smiled, Pops gave a slow approving nod, and the tension broke like a cloud clearing.

The grill smoked steady, ribs sizzling, sauce thick and sweet.
Moms' mac and cheese bubbled in the pan—golden, creamy, perfect. I'd dreamed about that meal for two years.

Later, Pops called everyone inside. When he used that tone, nobody questioned it. Moms, Maya, Dice, Nicole. The smell of barbecue clung to the air, sunlight spilling through the kitchen window like it used to on Sundays. For a moment, it almost felt like before.

We gathered around the table—me on one side, Dice on the other. Pops stood at the head, his presence still commanding, even with age softening the edges.

He cleared his throat.

"Now that I got both my boys' home, we gon' set some things straight," he said.

Dice shifted, avoiding my eyes. I kept mine down too, out of habit more than shame.

"I know what it's like to make mistakes that echo," Pops continued. "What y'all lived through... that's partly on me. I brought pain into this house when I stepped out on your mother. Thought I could handle it all and ended up handing y'all a war you never asked to fight."

Silence sat heavy, but it wasn't the kind that hurt. It was the kind that told the truth.

"But here's the thing," he said, voice steady. "Blood don't make you brothers—loyalty does. And loyalty doesn't mean blind. It means being honest, being accountable, being each other's keeper in the right way."

Moms reached for his hand; Maya squeezed mine under the table.

"I don't want to see no more distance between you two," Pops said. "You've both done your time—one behind bars, the other in his own mind. Now it's time to build something better. Together."

Dice looked at me then. Really looked.

"I'm trying," he said, voice quiet but real.
"I know," I told him. "We both learning."

Pops nodded.

"That's all I ask. Keep learning. Keep showing up. 'Cause the world's already hard enough, and the last thing a man needs is to fight his own blood."

He stood, his voice softening.

"When I'm gone, I need to know that y'all got each other's backs—not just when it's easy, but when it's ugly. That's what being your brother's keeper really means."

No one spoke for a while. Then Maya reached across the table, placing her hand over both mine and Dice's.

"Then I guess this is where we start," she said.

And just like that, for the first time in years, it felt like family again.

My Brother's Keeper

As the evening thinned out and people drifted back outside, Dice caught me near the garage. He looked like a different-older, maybe humbled.

"Man, I owe you," he said. "That day in the yard... I thought you were gonna let Trevor and his boys have me. I would've deserved it. But you didn't. You jumped in for me. That's when I finally got it—blood or not, you've been my brother longer than anyone."

For a second I couldn't speak. Then I laughed softly.

"I couldn't let that go down. You're my big brother. Always will be."

He nodded, eyes glassy, and pulled me into a hug.
It wasn't long or dramatic—just real. Years of tension, jealousy, and silence dropped away in that one embrace.

After Dice walked off, I stayed where I was for a minute, just watching. I looked around the yard—family, friends, and Maya's smile catching the evening light—and felt something settle in my chest. After all the fights, all the wrong turns, all the time lost, I finally had what I'd been searching for calmness.

Moms laughed from the porch, Pops flipped another slab on the grill, and Dice clapped me on the back like we'd been good all our lives. The smell of ribs and sweet smoke filled the air, heavy and familiar.

For the first time in forever, I didn't feel like I had to prove anything. I just belonged.

Hayzel Greene

Chapter Eighteen
The Clearing
Kid

Reporting to probation, I sat in the waiting area listening to the buzz of printers and the low hum of office chatter. The smell of burnt coffee and paper toner hung in the air—mundane, but steady. After everything, normal almost felt foreign.

My name was called.

"Andre Johnson."

I stood, the sound of it hitting differently now. My name had been used like a weapon before; today, I wanted to claim it back.

The officer at the door glanced up.

"Who are you here to see?"

"You. You called for Andre Johnson."

He frowned, looking me over, confusion flickering across his face.

"Yeah, but you're not the Andre Johnson in my case files."

I let out a slow breath, the kind that carried years of frustration.

"That's what I told them when they arrested me."

He motioned toward his office.

"Come inside. Let's sort this out."

Inside, the hum of the building faded. I sat across from him while he flipped through the folder, pages whispering like ghosts of what I'd been through. His brow furrowed, his eyes scanning back and forth until they finally stilled.

When he looked up, realization and a little shame had settled in.

"You're right," he said quietly. "You're not the one I had the warrant out for. You spent time for something your brother did."

I nodded once.

"Yeah. I told them that too. They had both of us locked up at the same time."

He shook his head, leaning back in his chair, that bureaucratic armor cracking just a little.

"I'll contact the court and get this cleared. I'm sorry, Mr. Johnson. You shouldn't have been there."

The words hung there. Simple. Heavy. You shouldn't have been there.

It didn't erase the time I'd lost, or the nights that reshaped me. But hearing someone finally say it out loud—it loosened something I didn't know I was still gripping.

I stood, shook his hand, and walked out into the sunlight. The air felt cleaner, the world quieter.

Name cleared. Record clean. Conscience steady.

For once, my story wasn't written by someone else's mistakes.
It was mine again.

Epilogue I

Kid

They say time changes a man. I don't think it does — it just shows you who you really are.

Two years gave me a front-row seat to my own lessons: what patience costs, what loyalty really means, and how love can outlast distance, bars, and bad decisions.

I walked in angry and came out free — not just from the system, but from the weight of proving myself. I learned that being your brother's keeper doesn't mean carrying his mess. It means knowing when to protect him, when to forgive him, and when to step out of the shadow of his choices.

Dice and I ain't perfect. We'll probably argue again, maybe even fall out again. But now we understand each other. That's enough.

And Maya... she stayed solid. Never wavered, never questioned. She taught me that love ain't about saving somebody — it's about standing still while they find their own way home.

I'm home now. And for the first time in a long time, I know exactly who I am.

Hayzel Greene

Epilogue II
Maya's Voice

Freedom looks good on him. It's in the way he walks now — shoulders lighter, eyes clear, laughter coming easy again. I watch him sometimes when he's not looking, just to remind myself this isn't a dream.

Two years of waiting, worrying, and praying taught me something too — that strength isn't about being loud; it's about showing up every day, even when it hurts.

There were nights I doubted, mornings I wanted to give up. But every letter he wrote back reminded me why I stayed. He never stopped being my somebody.

Now, when I smell his cologne drifting through the house or hear the low rumble of his bike pulling up outside, it hits me all over again — love this real don't fade. It just grows quiet, deeper, and more certain.

He told me once that patience was a test. Turns out, so is faith. And we passed both.

Hayzel Greene

The Quiet Between
Bridge between Part I & II

They say freedom hits differently when you've lost it. Maybe they're right. It's been months since they cleared my name, but sometimes I still wake up checking for bars, counting the seconds before the lights flicker on. I'll be halfway to the sink before I realize I'm not in that box anymore. The sound of running water ain't a trigger—it's a reminder. I made it out. But I brought some of it with me.

The funny thing about peace is—it doesn't come with the gate. You walk through that motherfucker, thinking you're free, and then realize your mind stayed behind. I guess that's what happens when you've been built to protect, to prove, to survive. My brother always said I made everything look easy. Truth is, I just got good at hiding what it cost.

Maya tries to remind me I'm home now. Dinner on the stove, candles lit, her laughter echoing through the house like music. But some nights, it's too quiet. The type of quiet that makes you face yourself. The kind that doesn't care how tough you are or how many stripes you earned.

Dice has been trying too. He called me almost every week now. Some days it feels normal—like we finally got it right. Other days, I hear the pause in his voice, that space where guilt still lives. I can't blame him. We both got blood on our hands, even if mine is from protecting and his is from pride.

Pops said time would fix it. But I'm learning time don't fix anything it just puts space between the hurt and the healing. The real work comes when you decide which one you want more.

I thought being my brother's keeper meant holding him down no matter what. Now I see it's about holding myself accountable, too. Sometimes peace costs more than loyalty, and forgiveness feels like work. But maybe that's what redemption really is—learning how to live without the armor.

So, I move slow now. Talk softer. Think before I swing. Don't mean I'm not still that same man. I just finally understand what my father meant when he said, *"Son, don't spend your whole life fighting battles that should've been conversations."*

This next part of my story ain't about proving I'm innocent. It's about staying that way. About building something that lasts longer than pain. About showing my brother that the blood between us ain't a curse, it's a choice.

And this time, I'm choosing stillness.

My Brother's Keeper:

The Price of Peace

Hayzel Greene

Prologue
The Gate Don't Close
Kid

They say freedom hits differently when you've been locked up. But nobody tells you it doesn't hit all at once.

When that gate slid open, it was quiet. No music, no cheers—just the sound of metal grinding against metal and a guard saying, *"You good to go."* That's it. Two years of my life, wrapped up in five words and a clang I can still hear in my sleep.

I stood there for a second longer than I should've. I didn't rush out. Didn't look back. Just stood still, feeling the cold hit my face and the heat roll off my chest. Freedom. Or at least that's what it was supposed to be.

But see… the thing about the gate is, it never really closes behind you. It follows. You walk out, but it walks with you. Every sound, every face, every piece of who you used to be—it stays tucked somewhere between your ribs, waiting to remind you you're not all the way free yet.

The world looked the same, but I didn't fit in it no more. Cars are too loud. People are too soft. Even the air felt heavier than I remembered. And maybe it wasn't the air—it was me. Carrying years of silence, guilt, and that same old story my pops wrote before I ever had a say in it.

Two women. Two sons. One man who couldn't keep his word. He started something and neither of us knew how to finish. Now I'm standing outside the gate, still trying to figure out how to close what he opened.

They tell you to move on, start over, be grateful you made it out. But what they don't tell you is—when you've been holding somebody else's sins long enough, they start to sound like your own. And that's a weight no gate can keep out.

So yeah… the gate don't close. Not really. It just changes shape. Turns into a front door, a phone call, a memory you can't shut down. And somewhere out here, on this side of the fence, I'm still learning how to walk through it.

Chapter One
Sunday Dinners
Kid

Sunday hit different when you've been gone a while. The smell of fried chicken, collard greens, and cornbread carried through the house like memory itself. That same hum of gospel low in the background, plates clinking, laughter spilling out from the kitchen. It used to sound like something simple. Now it sounded like something I was still trying to earn my way back into.

Moms was in her usual spot—apron on, slippers barely holding on her feet, scolding Pops for sneaking bites off the stove. Some things never changed. And maybe that's what scared me the most.

She looked up when she saw me in the doorway. "Boy, don't just stand there. Come fix you a plate before everything get gone."

That's how she said *welcome home*. No long speeches, no tears, just food and love. The only way she ever knew how.

Dice was there too sitting on the couch like nothing happened. Fresh fade, new chain, a smirk that didn't quite reach his eyes. I gave him a nod. He returned it. We were two men pretending our new relationship tasted better than it did.

We hadn't talked much since I got out. The air between us was still thick with everything we hadn't said. But family don't get to pick timing. Moms invited him, and he showed me. I guess that counted for something.

"Good to see you out, lil bro," he said, leaning back like we were cool.

"Yeah," I said, keeping my tone even. "Good to be out."

Pops caught my eye from across the table, that silence *don't start nothin'* look he'd been giving me since I was twelve. So, I sat down, broke bread, and kept it moving—for them.

For a while, it almost felt normal. The laughter, the stories, the way Moms fussed about second helpings like it was a sin to stop at one. But under it all, I could feel the shift. Everybody else had moved on. Jobs, bills, birthdays, and barbecues. I was the only one still catching up.

Later that night, when the dishes were done and the house got quiet, I stood outside on the porch. The night air was cool, the kind that made you remember who you used to be. Dice pulled up beside me, leaning on the rail like old times.

"I ain't never thanked you," he said after a minute. "For what you did inside."

I didn't answer right away. Just stared out at the streetlights stretching down the block like open wounds.

"You ain't have to," I finally said. "That's what brothers do, right?"

He nodded, slow. "Yeah. But it doesn't mean I deserved it."

I turned to look at him then; saw a piece of the kid he used to be hiding behind the man he became. For the first time, I wondered if maybe we both wanted the same thing—just didn't know how to say it.

Maybe calmness wasn't something you waited for. Maybe it was something you built; one uncomfortable Sunday at a time.

Chapter Two
The Offer
Kid

Two weeks out, and I was still getting used to silence that didn't come with locks. I woke up early, out of habit, sitting on the edge of the bed before the sun had even stretched. Maya was still asleep, her hair spilling across the pillow, breathing soft and steady. Calm looked good on her. I just wasn't sure how to wear it yet.

I had a job lined up—construction out in Euclid, nothing fancy but it kept my hands busy. Sweat and steel made sense to me; people didn't. Most days I come home too tired to think. But tiredness was better than angry. Better than lost.

Dice pulled up one evening in his black Charger, bass thumping before he even turned the corner. Same flash, same grin that always meant trouble dressed in confidence. I was sitting on the porch when he stepped out, chain catching the light like it had something to prove.

"What's good, lil bro?" he said, dap extended like the past never happened.

I stood, met him halfway. "Cooling. Just trying to stay out the way."

He laughed. "Man, you been out what—two weeks? You act like parole means hiding under a rock."

"Freedom mean keeping it," I said. "Ain't trying to go back."

Dice smirked; hands tucked in his pockets. "You always were the cautious one. But look, I got something for you. Something that'll put real money in your pocket."

That line hit old instincts. It smelled like the kind of opportunity that came with conditions. Still, I didn't move. Didn't say no either.

He went on, voice slick like a salesman: "Remember that old Inner Circle building? My people flipped it again. They are using the basement for private parties. VIP, no walk-ins. I need somebody to run it—security, keep things clean. You get a cut of the bar and the door. Easy money."

"Legal?" I asked, already knowing the answer.

Dice grinned wider. "It's… Cleveland legal."

I stared at him, the same way I used to when we were kids, and he'd talk me into doing something that ended with us both catching hell. "Nah, Dice. I'm good."

"Come on, Kid. You think you gonna stack enough working construction? That job ain't built for somebody like you. You a boss, always been."

I didn't like the way he said that like he was trying to remind me who I used to be. As he knew the fire still lived under my ribs.

"Bosses make better choices," I said. "That's the difference now."

For a second, I thought he'd drop it. Instead, he leaned back against the porch railing, eyes low. "You sound like Pops."

That hit differently. I didn't answer. Didn't have to. He knew what that name meant between us.

Dice sighed, pushed off the rail. "Aight, man. Offer stands if you change your mind." He started down the steps, then turned halfway. "Just remember—peace doesn't keep the lights on."

I watched his car pull away, the sound faded slowly. He wasn't wrong. But steadiness was the only thing I hadn't paid for yet.

Chapter Three
Maya's Quiet Storm
Maya

The first few weeks after Kid came home, I thought the absence of chaos had finally found us. He moved slower, talked softer, even smiled differently like the weight he carried had learned to sit quietly for once. But peace doesn't last when it's built on top of old wounds. It starts to crack where memory still bleeds.

At first, it was little things. The way he'd sit up in bed before the sun came up, elbows on his knees, breathing deep like he was still counting time. How he flinched every time the back gate creaked or when the phone rang after dark. Prison didn't just teach him discipline. It taught him how to disappear, even when he was standing right in front of me.

Dice had been coming around more too. Same loud laugh, same charm that didn't fool me. He brought noise with him — a reminder that calm was fragile and men like him didn't know how to handle it. I'd catch the two of them on the porch, talking in low tones. Every time Kid came back inside, he wore that look — the one caught between pride and regret. The one that made me hold my breath and pretend not to notice.

I wanted to ask what they talked about, but I didn't. Some questions don't fix things. They just make you part of the storm.

That night, Kid came in late. He didn't smell like liquor, but he smelled like old thoughts — the kind that follow you home when you don't want to be found. He stood in the doorway, shoulders tense, hands tucked in his hoodie pockets like he was keeping something from spilling.

"You good?" I asked.

He nodded once. "Yeah. Just thinking."

I set the towel down, crossed the room, and touched his arm. "Thinking don't mean carrying it alone, you know."

He gave a half-smile, that same one that used to melt me before it ever comforted me. "I'm good, Ma. Just tired."

He kissed my forehead and slipped past me toward the shower. The sound of running water filled the house, but my chest stayed loud.

From the window, I watched the streetlight bend against the mist. Everything looked calm, but I could feel something shifting in the air — that stillness before the clouds broke.

I didn't know what Dice had offered, or if Kid had said yes or no. All I knew was, a sense of oneness never comes without a fight... and something told me ours hadn't even started yet.

Chapter Four
Ghosts in the Mirror
Kid

There's something about mirrors that don't sit right with me anymore. Used to be, I'd pass one, flex, adjust my chain, keep it moving. Now, every time I catch my reflection, I see time looking back.

This morning was no different. Sunlight cut through the blinds, hitting that old mirror by the dresser — the one Maya wanted to replace but I told her to keep. I stared at it while brushing my teeth, watching my eyes move like they belonged to somebody else.

Same face. Same scars. But there was a different weight behind the look.

Two years in a cell don't just change how you see the world — it changes how you see yourself. Behind that glass, I could still see him. The version of me that swung first, that trusted too easily, that carried everyone else's mistakes like trophies. The brother who thought loyalty was enough to make wrongs right. The son who kept trying to fix what a man before him broke.

Sometimes I wonder if Pops knew what he left behind when he laid down with both those women. One decision split everything. Two sons born out of pride, both trying to live up to a man who never learned how to love either of them right. And now here we are — two grown men still fighting over the pieces.

I rinsed my face and looked up again. The mirror fogged, but the ghosts stayed clear. Dice's face flashed in my mind — that smirk that used to mean brotherhood, now just a reminder of everything blurred between us. He said peace doesn't pay bills. Maybe he was right. But what's the price of losing yourself trying to buy comfort?

I reached for my shirt and paused, staring one last time before walking away. The man looking back didn't flinch, didn't fold — but he didn't look free either.

That's when I realized something heavy: Prison taught me how to survive without walls—but not how to live outside of them.

Later that night, Maya found me sitting at the edge of the bed, staring at nothing. "You still thinking about Dice?" she asked, her voice soft but sure.

I shook my head. "Thinking about everything."

She didn't press. Just sat beside me, her hand finding mine. For a moment, I thought maybe that was enough — that her quiet was stronger than all my noise.

But in the back of my mind, I still heard that gate slam. And I knew — nothing wasn't going to come easy. Not for me. Not for us. Not while ghosts still looked like family.

Chapter Five
Dice's Slip
Kid

It was a Wednesday night when the call came through. Maya was in the kitchen, music low, humming to herself while she packed lunch for the morning. I was half-watching the game, half-counting the hours since I'd last heard from Dice.

He'd been quiet. Too quiet. And silence from Dice never meant resolve—it meant planning.

When I saw his name flash across my phone, I hesitated. Three rings before I picked up.

"Yo."

"Kid, you home?" His voice was too calm, the kind that already knew the answer to the question it was asking.

"Yeah. What's good?"

A pause. Then, "Need a favor."

That sentence — those two words — had already cost me too much. Still, I said, "What kind of favor?"

"Nothing wild. Just come through. Circle."

The Circle. Same old spot from back in the day. That alone told me whatever this was, it wasn't clean.

Maya caught my eye from across the room, reading the shift in my body before I said a word. "Everything okay?" she asked.

I nodded, lying through my teeth. "Yeah. Just Dice."

She stared a second longer, then said quietly, "Be careful, Kid. You been home too short to risk it."

Her voice lingered even after the door shut behind me.

The lot behind the old Inner Circle building was dim, just one flickering streetlight holding the darkness back. Dice's Charger was there, door cracked, smoke trailing from the window like a warning. I approached him slowly.

He leaned back in the driver's seat, phone in one hand, counting a small stack of cash with the other.

"What's this?" I asked.

"Relax," he said, grinning. "It ain't what it looks like."

"Then tell me what it is."

He smirked, flicked the rubber band off the stack. "Business."

I laughed, no humor in it. "Same kind of business that had me doing time for you?"

His smile dropped. "You still on that?"

"Till the day I stop breathing," I said. "You cost me two years of my life, Dice. You think I just forget that because we broke bread?"

He sighed, leaned forward. "You think I meant for that to happen? I was trying to fix it. They ran your name by mistake."

"Stop lying."

"Kid—"

"Nah. I'm done being your clean-up crew."

My Brother's Keeper

He looked away then, tapping the wheel with his thumb. "You sound like Pops."

There it was again. The animosity of his childhood trauma displayed angrily.

"Don't do that," I warned.

"I'm just saying… he left both of us with scraps. You built something outta yours. I'm still trying to find mine."

I took a step closer, voice low. "Finding yours don't mean taking mine with it."

For a second, the only sound was the hum of the streetlight. Then Dice laughed — not the kind that came from humor, but from hurt.

"You always thought you was better than me."

"No," I said, steady. "Just tried to be different."

He nodded slowly, eyes cold now. "Different don't last in this city."

That's when I saw it — the bag on the passenger seat. Not money. Not clothes. **Weight.** Small enough to hide. Big enough to ruin him.

I exhaled, long and tired. "You still playing with the same fire."

Dice stared straight ahead. "Fire's the only thing that ever kept me warm."

I walked away that night, heat in my chest, words in my throat that I didn't trust myself to say. Didn't sleep. Didn't tell Maya. Because sometimes, love doesn't need to hear the details — it just needs to survive them.

But in the pit of my stomach, I knew one thing for sure: If Dice went down again, he wouldn't be going alone this time—and somehow, I already knew whose name would get called.

Chapter Six
The Crossroads
Kid

The next few days stretched long and restless. Maya could feel it before I said a word. She could tell I was under pressure.

Dice's business was his, but it always found a way to bleed into mine. Even after I walked away from that parking lot, the sound of his voice followed me like an echo I couldn't shake. *Fire's the only thing that ever kept me warm.* That line hit me harder than I wanted to admit.

Friday afternoon, I was just getting off work when two unmarked cars rolled up slowly to the curb. You learn to spot them — the kind that don't belong but act like they do. Windows down. One of the detectives leaned out, the other stayed watching my hands.

"Mr. Johnson?" the driver said, flashing a badge I didn't ask to see.

"What's this about?"

"Your brother," he said, like it explained everything. "You got a minute?"

That was the problem—I had too many minutes and not enough reasons to say no.

We stepped aside, his voice low and polite like a man trying to make you comfortable before cutting deep.

"There was a disturbance near the Circle last night. Your brother's name came up. Yours too."

I laughed under my breath. "I wasn't there."

"Good," he said, nodding. "Let's keep it that way."

His tone had a warning in it. Not a threat — a favor. Then he handed me a card. "In case you hear from him."

They pulled off slowly, leaving dust in the air and a familiar weight in my chest.

When I got home, Maya was on the porch, eyes already reading mine. "What happened?" she asked before I sat down.

"Nothing," I said, rubbing my hands together. "Just the past showing up again."

She didn't speak right away, just leaned back in the chair beside me. "Kid, you can't keep carrying him. You love him, I get it. But love doesn't mean dying slow beside him."

I didn't answer, couldn't. She was right but right doesn't always feel possible.

I looked out at the street; the same one we used to ride through when life was loud and easy. Now it felt small — like no matter how far I drove, I'd still end up right back here.

"I keep thinking if I just talk to him, maybe he'll listen," I said finally.

Maya turned to me. "And if he doesn't?"

I didn't have an answer for that either.

That night, I drove. No destination, just movement. Streetlights slid over the hood like slow confession. The city looked the same — cracked corners, faded murals, storefronts still hustling survival. Everything stayed moving, even when it was broken.

I pulled up to the lake. Parked. Rolled the window down. The air smelled like memory — salt, smoke, and old promises. For the first time, I wondered if maybe being calm wasn't about choosing between loyalty and freedom. Maybe it was about learning how to let one die without burying the other.

The waves hit hard against the rocks, rhythmic, endless. I closed my eyes and let the sound work through me. Somewhere between the crash and the silence, I heard my father's voice — low, tired, the one he used when he knew he'd done wrong.

Be your brother's keeper, Kid… but don't lose yourself keeping him.

When I opened my eyes again, I knew what I had to do. The crossroads wasn't between right and wrong anymore, it was between staying stuck or finally choosing myself.

Hayzel Greene

Chapter Seven
The Choice
Kid

I found Dice two nights later. Same corner, same crowd — different kind of danger. The music was loud, bass spilling through busted speakers while people drifted in and out of the alley like ghosts with somewhere to be.

He was leaning against the wall, phone in hand, head down. I didn't even see me walk up until my shadow touched his shoes.

"Yo," I said.

He looked up, startled at first, then smiled. "Damn, you move quiet these days."

"Had to learn that inside," I said. "Noise get you noticed."

He smirked, pocketed the phone. "You here to preach or play?"

"Neither" I said. "I'm here to finish what we started."

That got his attention. He pushed off the wall, stood straight. "What's that supposed to mean?"

"It means I can't keep watching you crash and pretending I ain't standing too close."

He laughed — short, bitter. "You think you my savior now? Man, you ain't gotta fix me."

"I'm not trying to fix you, Dice," I said. "I'm trying to keep us both alive."

His smile faded, replaced by that hard stare that used to freeze me when we were kids. "You don't get it. You made it out. You got your girl, your clean job, and your little happiness. But I'm not built for that. Some of us only know how to survive in chaos."

"Then learn something new," I snapped.

He shook his head slowly. "You sound like Pops again."

"Maybe he was right about something," I said. "Maybe being your brother's keeper don't mean holding you up when you keep trying to fall."

That hit him. I saw it in his eyes — that flicker of guilt he never let last long.

He looked away, mumbling, "You ain't built for this life no more, Kid."

"Good," I said. "Because I'm done living it."

I took a step back, voice lower now. "Cops came to see me. Said your name was in their mouth again. You need to handle your business or turn yourself in before they handle it for you.

He froze. "You talked to them?"

"I didn't have to. They already watching."

Silence filled the space between us. Then Dice smiled, "not the good kind. "Guess you finally picked a side."

I sighed, the weight in my chest turning sharp. "There was never supposed to be sides. Just brothers."

He took a step closer, eyes hard. "You gonna run to them when they come knocking again?"

I met his stare. "I'm gonna protect what's mine. Whatever that means."

He studied me, jaw tight. "You really think you can walk away from this?"

My Brother's Keeper

"I already did," I said. "Now it's on you."

For a long moment, neither of us spoke. Then he nodded — slow, like a man walking into his own fate. "Alright, little bro. I guess this is where the road splits."

"Been splitting," I said softly.

He turned to go, that familiar swagger still in his step, but it looked heavier now — like he finally knew what it cost.

I stood there until the alley went quiet again, until his shadow disappeared around the corner. Then I exhaled, the sound breaking like something leaving my body for good.

Maybe blood made us brothers. But peace made me free.

Hayzel Greene

Chapter Eight
Light
Maya

Calmness doesn't come easy. Not the kind that lasts, anyway. It creeps in quiet, testing if you've really made room for it or if you're still saving space for the storm.

Kid had been different lately. Calmer—but not the kind that comes from rest. The kind that comes from release. He stopped pacing at night. Stopped looking out the window like something was coming for him. The sound of his keys on the dresser every evening became my new comfort, a small reminder that he made it home again.

We didn't talk about Dice. Not after that last time. But I knew something in him had shifted. The look in his eyes was clearer — the same eyes that used to carry everybody's weight but his own. Now, they looked lighter. Still guarded. Still watchful. But lighter.

One morning, I woke up before him. The sunlight stretched across his back, tracing the scars the world couldn't see. I watched his chest rise slowly, steady. No tension. No twitch. Just breath. It felt like the first time I'd seen him sleep in peace since he came home.

I got up, made coffee, cracked the window to let the breeze in. The world smelled like something starting over — fresh rain, cut grass, the faint hum of traffic. I didn't know if it was hope or just habit, but it felt good to breathe without checking for warning signs.

When he finally came into the kitchen, he smiled at me — a real one this time. The kind that reached his eyes. "Morning," he said, voice rough from sleep.

"Morning," I said back, handing him a mug. "You slept long."

"Yeah." He took a sip, leaned against the counter. "Felt different."

"Different good?"

He nodded. "Different right."

I smiled at that. "Maybe peace finally decided to stay a while."

He looked at me then, that slow, deep look that made time go quiet. "If it did," he said, "it's because you kept the light on."

I didn't answer. Just reached out and touched his hand. Warm. Solid. Real.

Sometimes love ain't about saving somebody — it's about standing still while they find their own way back. And at that moment, with morning light spilling across the table and his fingers brushing mine, I knew we'd both finally found it.

It wasn't perfect. But it was ours.

Chapter Nine
The Turning
Kid

Life has a funny way of testing you — right when you start trusting it.

A month had passed since I last saw Dice. No calls. No texts. No drop-ins with that grin that used to mean trouble. At first, I kept waiting for it — some words from the streets, some knock at the door in the middle of the night. But nothing came. And sometimes nothing is louder than anything.

Work was steady. Maya was steady. Life was… simple. And I didn't realize how much I missed simple until I had it again.

Then, one evening, I was walking out of the hardware store when I saw him. Dice. Standing across the street, hands in his pockets, just watching. For a second, I thought maybe I imagined him — the sun hitting that same chain, his stance too familiar to mistake.

He didn't call out. Didn't cross. Just nodded once. And in that small motion, I saw everything he couldn't say — apology, pride, and distance.

I nodded back. That was it. No words. No promises. Just two brothers standing on opposite sides of the same street, finally letting go without saying goodbye.

When I got home, Maya was lighting candles, music low. She looked up and smiled. "You good?"

"Yeah," I said, taking off my jacket. "Think I finally turned a corner."

She raised an eyebrow. "That right?"

"Yeah. Feels different now."

She walked over, slid her arms around my waist. "Different right?"

"Different right," I repeated, smiling against her hair.

Outside, the wind picked up — not harsh, just steady, like the city was exhaling. For the first time, I didn't feel like I had to watch my back. It didn't feel like I owed anybody my happiness.

Maybe that's what turning really meant —not forgetting where you came from, just deciding not to keep driving the same road.

Chapter Ten
The Keeper's Code
Kid

People like to throw that phrase around — *be your brother's keeper.* But nobody ever explains what it really costs.

They don't tell you how heavy that kind of love can get. How it'll pull at you from both sides until you forget which one you belong to. How sometimes, doing right by somebody means walking away before they drag you under.

For a long time, I thought being my brother's keeper meant protecting him no matter what. Taking his hits. Cleaning his mess. Carrying blame so he could breathe easily. But all that did was teach him how to fall without ever learning how to stand.

Now I understand — keeping your brother doesn't mean saving him. It means holding space for him to change, even if he never does. It means knowing when to love him from a distance.

There's a difference between carrying someone and covering them. Carrying breaks, you. Covering gives you both a chance to heal.

I still think about Dice sometimes. Wonder if he's alright. Wonder if he ever figured out what unconditional acceptance feels like. But I don't chase those thoughts no more. Because love doesn't always need to be loud. Sometimes it's quiet — steady — a prayer whispered under your breath and left in God's hands.

Some mornings I wake up and the house is quiet in a way that doesn't scare me. Maya hums while she moves around, coffee brewing, light slipping in through the windows. No sirens. No shadows. Just a life that feels earned. And when I think about Dice, it's not with anger anymore. It's with hope—from a distance. That's as close as I can love him now. And that's enough.

Maya once told me peace doesn't find you until you stop fighting for control. Maybe she was right. Maybe keeping my brother wasn't about what I did for him—but about what I finally did for myself.

So yeah — I'm still my brother's keeper. Just not his savior. That's the code now.

Epilogue I
The Ride Home
Kid

The road out of the city looked different now. Not cleaner, not brighter — just calmer. The kind of calm that doesn't ask for permission to exist.

Maya had her hand out the window, catching the wind like she used to when we first started riding together. The sun was low, washing everything in gold. It hit her skin just right — soft, steady, unbothered. Every now and then, she'd look over and smile that small, knowing smile that said everything without saying a word.

We didn't have a destination. Just somewhere past familiar. Past noise. Past history.

For the first time, I didn't feel the need to rush. I didn't feel like I was running from or to anything. Just *here*. Just Breathing.

The radio played something old — EPMD again. The same track from Gordon Park all those years ago. Funny how life cycles back like that. Back then, I was living loud, chasing respect, carrying everyone's weight like it proved something. Now, I just wanted quite strong enough to drown out the past.

Maya reached over, laced her fingers through mine. "You alright?" she asked.

"Yeah," I said, eyes on the road. "For the first time, I think I am."

She nodded, turned her face back toward the wind. "Then let's keep driving."

The highway stretched ahead, endless and open — like forgiveness. And for once, I didn't look back.

Hayzel Greene

Epilogue II
Peace
Maya

The night settled quiet after the drive. The kind of quiet that doesn't need filling.

Kid fell asleep before the credits rolled on the movie we weren't watching. I stayed awake, tracing the shape of his hand against mine — rough, warm, real.

For years I'd prayed for him to come home, then prayed for peace to stay once he did. Funny how you don't realize the difference between the two until both finally show up.

He used to carry everything — guilt, anger, the weight of his brother, his father, even me. Now he just carried breath. Slow, even, easy.

I turned toward him and whispered what I never got the chance to say when the world was louder: "You kept your promise. You made it home."

He didn't move, but I swear he heard me — the way his shoulders eased told me so.

Outside, the moonlight spilled across the window, soft and patient. No more gates. No more waiting. Just us. Here. Whole.

Peace ain't something that finds you. It's something you decide to live in. And tonight, we finally did.

Hayzel Greene

For the Reader

Every story I tell starts with a heartbeat. Sometimes it's fast and wild, sometimes it's slow and heavy — but it's always real.

My Brother's Keeper came from a place between silence and survival — that space where love and loyalty don't always look the same. I wanted to write about the kind of men we don't always understand and the kind of women who love them anyway. The ones who carry too much, forgive too often, and learn too late that peace is a choice, not a prize.

This story isn't about right or wrong. It's about the weight of what we inherit and the courage it takes to lay it down. About blood that binds and burdens. About family — the kind that breaks you, builds you, and still calls you home.

To anyone who's ever had to choose between love and peace, I see you. To anyone learning to forgive what was never theirs to fix, I feel you. And to the ones still holding the light for somebody who's trying to find their way — keep shining. Sometimes that's the only way home.

Thank you for riding with me through both parts of this story — *A Story of Blood and Redemption* and *The Price of Peace*. Every word was written with truth, love, and a little Cleveland grit.

Until the next one…

– Hayzel Greene

Stories that linger long after the last page.

Hayzel Greene

ABOUT THE AUTHOR

Hayzel Greene is a storyteller, screenwriter, and author who thrives at the crossroads of love, truth, and transformation. Her work explores the messy beauty of connection where humor, heartbreak, and healing met.

Through her brand, **The HG Collection**, Hayzel continues to build worlds that resonate with authenticity and emotion. From her film *Flower: A Dope Girl's Story* to her romantic fiction projects like *Beyond the Dare* and *Caught in the Setup*, her stories are unapologetically real.

When she's not writing, Hayzel pours her creativity into community storytelling, audio production, and mentorship through her *Ink to Impact* initiative.

Her voice is distinct, her style grounded, and her stories linger long after the last page.

Follow Hayzel Greene and The HG Collection for more real, raw, and unapologetic stories.

Hayzel Greene

OTHER WORKS BY HAYZEL GREENE

COMING SOON

Flower: A Dope Girl's Story (Film)

Lost in My Favorite Romance Novel

    (A story where the reader becomes the story)

The Sound Between Us

The Haven Series

Also published by Hayzel Greene

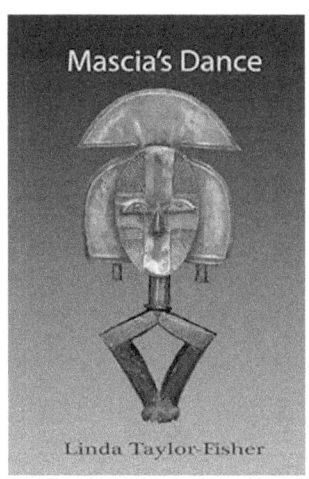

www.ingramcontent.com/pod-product-compliance
Lightning Source LLC
Chambersburg PA
CBHW051346020726
47501CB00007B/2302